DISNEY'S
HERCULES
I Made Herc a Hero

by Phil

Gabrielle Charbonnet

DISNEY
PRESS

New York

Printed in Mexico.

ISBN: 0-7868-4116-8

Contents

Read all the Disney Chapters!

Other Exciting Books Based on Hercules

Chapter One

Pleased to Meet Ya

 Hi! Philoctetes here. Call me Phil. Everyone does. Lately people have been asking about my Wonder Boy, Hercules. All day long, it's Herc this and Herc that. So here's the straight story, once and for all.

By now everyone knows that Hercules' real parents were the gods Zeus and Hera, but he'd spent eighteen years on earth harvesting olives for his mortal mom and pop. That's because when Herc was just a baby, Hades, party-pooper god of the underworld, had made him mortal.

1

Hades had been trying to knock Herc off, see, so that he wouldn't get in the way when Hades made his move to take over Mount Olympus. But at the time none of us, not even Zeus, knew what Hades was plotting.

Anyway, you might have noticed I'm part man and part goat. So I'm a satyr. Big deal. In my day, I was just about the hottest coach around.

I trained the best: Achilles, Jason, Odysseus, you name him. But every one of those guys let me down. Not one went the distance. So I gave up.

Can you blame me? I retired to a little island paradise, Idra. And I was happy there: just me and my memories.

So one day I was outside, minding my own business, when *wham*! Out of the blue sky came a guy on—get this—a flying horse. The guy was just a kid—a big, clumsy, humongously strong kid.

He said, "Hey. Are you Phil?"

"That's right," I said.

He grabbed my hand and practically crushed the bones. "Boy, am I glad to meet you. I'm Hercules."

Well, I didn't know Hercules from a hole in the ground.

"I need your help!" said the kid. "I want to become a true hero."

"Sorry, kid," I said. "No can do. I'm not in the hero-training business any more, all right?" Then I hightailed it into my little hut.

The last thing I needed was to be let down by some starry-eyed yahoo with more muscles than brains. I'd had my hopes stomped on before.

The kid hollered outside my door. "Wait! I've got to do this. Haven't you ever had a dream? Something you just *had* to do?"

I snorted. Who did he think he was talking to? I yanked open my door. "Yeah, kid, I had a dream," I snarled. "I dreamed I was going to train the greatest hero there was. So

great, the gods would hang a picture of him in the stars, for everyone to see. And people would look at it and say, 'Hey, that's Phil's boy.'"

"What happened?" the kid asked.

"None of them—Jason, Achilles, Odysseus—went the distance!" I said. "Look, dreams are for rookies. Now, forget about it."

"I'm different from those other guys!" said the kid. "I can do it, Phil. Come on, I'll show you!"

So he tried to impress me. The kid picked up a huge chunk of statue and threw

it into the sea.

I didn't impress easily. "Very nice," I said. "So you're strong.

So are a million other guys. So what?"

The kid looked disappointed. "But if I don't become a true hero," he said, "I'll never be able to rejoin my father, Zeus, on Mount Olympus."

Hello! I skidded to a halt, both hooves planted in the ground. "Your father is *Zeus*?" I shouted. And I thought, maybe there's more to this kid than a couple of big biceps.

Chapter Two

From Zero to Hero

Well! Having Zeus, Mr. Lightning Bolts, for a father made all the difference. We're talking bonafide *god* here. I decided to get my gear out of mothballs and take the kid on. After all, if anyone could mold this overgrown farm boy into something, it was me, Phil, trainer to some of the most famous names in the history scrolls.

"Okay, kid," I said. "I'll do it."

"Great!" the kid gushed. "You won't be

sorry, Phil. So when do we start? Can we start now?"

Talk about eager. The way this kid acted, I could almost believe he would come through for me. But first things first. We gave his flying horse, Pegasus, some oats and some birdseed. Then we began.

"The main thing," I said, "is control. Sure, you've got muscles, but your aim is nowhere."

Hercules nodded.

"Next," I said, "is smarts. It's not enough to be able to rescue someone. You've got to know *when* and *how* to do it. You can't just leap into things. We've got to work on that."

"Sure thing," said the kid.

"But first, let's get you toned up." I started the kid on a strict training schedule—aerobics, weights, you name it. Day in, day out, it was Phil's Famous Fitness Program.

Time passed. Herc grew stronger and bigger, if you can believe it. Pegasus helped out with Herc's exercises.

Finally I started to see some progress.
The kid was coming along. But would he go
the distance? I couldn't tell. After many
months of my expert training, advice, and
hard work, he faced one final do-or-die test.
But he was cocky.

"Ha!" Hercules said. "I passed all your tests, Phil! I'm ready for herodom, I can feel it."

"All right, take it easy, champ," I said. "Don't get your toga in a twist."

"But I'm ready!" the kid insisted. "I want to get off this island. I want to battle some monsters and rescue some damsels. You know, heroic stuff. Then—next stop, Olympus."

I gave in. "Okay, kid. We'll take the show on the road. Saddle Pegasus. We're going to Thebes."

Chapter Three

Meeting Megara

Herc and yours truly were on Pegasus's back, flying toward Thebes like a bat out of Hades, when we heard someone screaming.

"Sounds like your basic D.I.D.," I said. "Damsel in Distress. Go to it, Herc."

We swooped down. This would be a good test for the kid, his first real, damsel rescue. I got ready to grade him on approach, method, and follow-through.

The damsel was being chased by a big blockheaded centaur.

"I like them feisty," the centaur chuckled, grabbing her.

I could see Herc was steaming mad.

I frowned at him. Rule seven is "Don't get too involved." But the kid had never seen a girl like this one before.

"Now, remember," I whispered. "Analyze the situa—"

But the kid had already leaped right into the centaur's path. I took points off his grade for that.

"Halt!" said Herc.

12

"Take a hike, two-legs," snarled the centaur.

"Yeah, back off, Atlas," said the girl.

Hercules blinked. "Uh, aren't you a
damsel in distress?"

"I'm a damsel," she panted, wrestling
with the centaur. "I'm in distress. I can handle this. Have a nice day."

I groaned from the sidelines. Great. An
independent type.

"I think you need help," said Herc stubbornly.

Next thing you know, *wham!* With the girl still in his clutches, the centaur kicked Herc halfway across the river. I took points off for that, too.

"Get your sword, Herc!" I yelled.

But the centaur already had the jump on him. The kid was getting slammed into rocks, dunked in the water, you name it. He'd forgotten everything I'd ever taught him!

"Concentrate!" I shouted. "Use your head!" and he did—Herc butted the centaur's stomach. Not exactly what I'd had in mind. . . .

Finally the centaur dropped the girl, and Herc seemed to get a grip on the situation. His training kicked in. He started fighting for real. Soon Herc was beating the hay out of the the centaur. With a huge one-two punch Herc knocked him right off his hooves. *Wham!*

14

"Way to go, Herc!" I called.

Herc swaggered over to us. "How was that, Phil?" he asked cockily. "I beat him!"

"You lost a lot of points, kid," I said sternly. "You were sloppy, you didn't think, you got distracted by a pair of big blue eyes, . . ."

The kid wasn't even listening. "Are you all right, miss?" he asked the girl.

"I'm fine," she said. "I was fine even before you helped. My name's Megara, by the way."

I was getting a bad feeling about Meg, but I couldn't put my hoof on it. Herc was

drooling over the girl like he was starving and she was a pita sandwich.

"I'm . . . I'm," stammered the kid.

"Yes?" said Megara. "You *do* have a name, don't you?"

"My name is Hercules," he blurted. "Can

we give you a lift somewhere?"

Pegasus snorted, and I couldn't blame him. The kid was making a fool of himself over a girl we didn't know from Pandora.

Megara looked at Pegasus, sizing up the situation. She was a sharp one. "That's all right," she said. "I'm a big girl. Thanks, anyway, Wonder Boy." Then she took off down the road toward Thebes.

Herc started after her. "Wow," he said.

"She's really something isn't she, Phil?"

"Yeah," I snarled. "She's a real pain in the tail. Now snap back to reality! We got a job to do, remember?"

"Oh, right, right," said Herc. "Thebes."

Pegasus and I rolled our eyes at each other. The kid had a long way to go.

Chapter Four

Thebes, the Big Olive

You know what they say about Thebes nowadays: If you can make it there, you can make it anywhere. But back then Thebes was a big accident waiting to happen. There was plenty of action for a boy who wanted to become a hero.

When we got to town, Herc's country-boy eyes were popping out of his head.

"Gosh," he said. "There are so many people here. So many chariots and carts and people selling stuff. . . ."

"Stick close, kid," I told him. "The city is a dangerous place." I grabbed his arm, saving him from being run down by a chariot. "I'm walking here!" I shouted at the driver. "Wacko!"

"Hey, kid," a shady voice whispered. "Wanna buy a sundial?"

I yanked Hercules away from the guy. "Just stare at the sidewalk," I told Herc.

"People here are nuts. This town's gone downhill, which is good for us, 'cause it means they need a hero. Right?"

"Uh, right," said Herc, his eyes wide.

"Now, all we need is some kind of disaster," I said, rubbing my hands together. "A volcano would be good. Or a monster of some kind. Dragon, cyclops, something like that."

Hercules sighed. "I can do it, Phil. I just need one chance to show these people I can be a hero."

"Help! Please, somebody help! There's been a terrible accident!"

Herc brightened. I narrowed my eyes. Where had I heard that voice before? Then Megara burst through the crowd.

"Help!" she cried.

"Meg?" Hercules said happily.

Pegasus and I were both suspicious. What was she doing here? How could she be in trouble *again*?

"Hercules, thank goodness!" Meg said.

"Quick, right outside of town. Two little boys, playing in a gorge . . . there was a rock slide . . . you've got to help!
They're trapped!"

"All right!"
Hercules punched the air. "This is great! Come on!" He grabbed Meg and hauled her onto Pegasus's back. Pegasus did *not* look thrilled. They took off.

"Oh, don't worry about me," I called after him. "I'll get there all right." Sheesh—talk about gratitude! I trotted behind them, heading out of town. The rest of Thebes was right behind me.

* * *

Hercules was already doing his hero stuff
when I arrived, gasping for breath. A crowd
had gathered. Two boys were crying for help.

It was child's play for Herc—he shifted a humongous boulder out of the way, and the boys scampered out. Meg stared at Herc.

"All right!" I yelled, clapping hard. But the crowd wasn't impressed. They were going to be a tough sell.

"Gee, thanks, mister," said one boy.

"Yeah. You're really strong," said the other boy.

"Try to be more careful next time, okay, kids?" said Herc.

"We sure will," said the first one. And they ran off.

"Wow, Phil, I did great!" said Herc, all puffed up and sure of himself. "Listen, the folks are still applauding."

I listened. It wasn't applause I was hearing. It was more of a . . . hissing. A *hissing?*

"Uh, kid," I said. "I hate to burst your bubble, but . . ." I pointed to the cave.

When Herc had moved the boulder, he had uncovered the cave's mouth. The hissing got louder. As Herc and I watched, a huge, ugly, dragonlike monster slithered out of the dark opening. The crowd scattered.

"Uh, what do you call that thing?" Herc asked.

"Sir! Your majesty! Anything it *wants*!" I said, then ran and hid behind a rock. Hey, I just *train* heros, I never said I was a hero *myself*.

Now, you read all about Herc's battle with the Hydra in the newstablets, so I won't bore you with the details. We all know that when Herc cut off the thing's head, three new heads grew in its place. That wasn't a big deal.

But when Herc cut off those, *boom*, it had nine heads. Then it got sticky. To tell you the truth, it looked touch and go for a while.

I mean, this Hydra thing was big, and it meant business. I had taught Herc every trick in the book, but who expected a Hydra to pop up out of nowhere?

Finally, Herc buried it—and himself— under a mountain of rocks. Bang. End of the Hydra. I thought it was the end of Herc, too, but he crawled out, alive. The crowd went wild. Hercules had finally impressed them.

"You did it, kid!" I yelled. "Now, *that* was heroic!"

Chapter Five

One Hero, At Your Service

From then on, Herc was so hot, steam looked cool next to him. You name the problem, Hercules could solve it. A giant boar, harpies, a sea monster? No problem. Herc was going the distance for me. It was fabulous. The people thought he was the best thing since they put the pocket in pita.

Meanwhile I had my hands full, dealing with all the people who wanted to make money off Hercules' name. . . . I'd never worked so hard in my life. We had Herc action figures, Herc sandals, Herculade drinks. . . . We were living the good life, and it was fine.

But somehow it wasn't enough. Herc had checked with his dad, Zeus, and Zeus told him he wasn't a real hero yet. Sheesh, Herc was doing great. What was Zeus's problem?

Just last week Herc had made mincemeat of a minotaur and the crowds had gone crazy. But Zeus wanted Herc to look inside his heart,whatever that meant.

One day I came home and found Herc all mopey-faced.

"Yo, kid," I said. "Glad I caught you. Let's update your schedule. At noon today you have a meeting with King Augeus—some kind of problem with his stable. Then at one we're seeing some Amazons—"

"Yeah, yeah," said Herc. "But what's the point? I mean, where is all this getting me?"

Zeus's talk had really thrown him. "Kid, you can't give up now!" I said.

"Look, I've given it everything I had," said Herc sadly. "I just don't know what else I can do."

The kid was *down*. "Listen to me," I told him. "I've seen them all. They come and they go. But this is the honest-to-

29

Zeus truth, kid. You got something I've never seen before. There's *nothing* you can't do."

"Really?" Herc asked. "You think so?"

"Hey. Would I lie to you?" I said.

Just then, in the middle of our pep talk, a swarm of tourists burst into the room.

"Quick!" I said. "Emergency escape plan."

"Okay!" Herc agreed.

While the kid ducked behind a curtain, I created a diversion out on the patio. "Over here!" I yelled. "I see him by that fountain!"

I almost got stampeded. When it was quiet, I went back inside. What Herc was doing was good—I had to make him see that.

But when I got back, the kid was nowhere to be found. He had disappeared without a trace.

Chapter Six

Who is Meg, Anyway?

I almost went nuts. A star like Herc, out without an escort? He could get kidnapped, he could get mugged. . . . Then I remembered it was *Hercules* we were talking about. It'd take major muscle to harm him. Still, where did he go? I was worried sick, and so was Pegasus.

The two of us searched, but didn't see a single sandal print. Finally, that night, we found him in a garden, yakking away with —you guessed it—that Megara girl. I defi-

32

nitely did *not* trust her.

"All right!" I yelled. "Break it up! Party's over!"

"I've been looking all over for you, kid!" I snapped at Hercules. "Did you ever think I might be *worried*? Not to mention you stood up some important business contacts. Like the *Amazons*, for example. You know what happens when you get an Amazon mad? Well, let me tell you—"

"Okay, mutton man, we get the picture," said Meg. "Don't blame Herc. It was all my fault."

I pointed at her. "You're already on my list, sister. Don't make it worse." I turned back to Herc. "And you! You're going to the stadium right now! You better go put in the best workout of your life, you hear me? And another thing—"

"Got it, Phil," said the kid.

"I'm sorry, Wonder Boy," said Meg.

"He'll get over it," Herc said, handing her

a flower.

I clapped my hands. "Move, move, move, move!"

Herc and I climbed back on Pegasus. But the lovesick fool wasn't watching where he was going. Next thing I knew, I was flat on my back in a briar patch, watching Pegasus's tail sail off into the sky. That did it! *Now* I was mad.

I picked myself up and dusted off my fur. It would be a long trot home.

I hadn't gone very far when I heard the voices. A guy and a girl off to the side of the road. The girl was Meg! I hid and listened.

"Meg, Meg, Meg," said the guy. "Don't forget that you owe me."

"Look, Hades," said Meg. "I've been thinking . . . "

My pointy little ears practically caught fire. Hades! Low-down god of the underworld. *Meg* was pals with him!

"Leave the think-

35

ing to me," said Hades. "I'm telling you I want Wonder Boy. You're going to get him for me, right? Right?"

Wonder Boy? Hercules! Well, I'd heard all I needed to. I slipped away and ran for home as fast as my hooves could take me.

I burst into the stadium, where Herc was still working out. He had this goofy, dreamy

smile on his face. I knew what it meant: trouble. The kid thought he was in love. And I was going to have to burst his bubble. I had to break it to him gently.

"Phil!" yelled Herc. He grabbed me and swung me around. "Phil, I had the greatest day! Meg is fantastic! I can't stop thinking about her. Don't you think she's amazing?"

"Yeah," I said. "Sure. Listen, kid, calm down for a second. We got to talk."

"I know you're upset about today," Herc broke in.

"Look, that's not the point," I began.

"The point is, I love her!" said Herc.

"The point is, she's a two-timing weasel! She's been lying to you!" I yelled. Okay, okay, so I forgot the

37

gentle part. "All this time, she's been playing footsie with Hades. They're planning to bring you down, kid!"

"You're lying!" the kid roared.

"I heard her!" I roared back. Then, *boom*! I was sailing across the stadium. The kid had taken a poke at me! At *me*, who had made him everything he was. Me, who had done so much for him.

I picked myself up and dusted off my fur for the second time that night. "Fine," I said. "I've had enough."

"Phil, I'm sorry," stammered Herc.

"You won't listen to the truth," I said coldly. "I'm hopping on the first barge out of here. I'm going home!"

"Fine! Go!" said Herc. "I don't need you."

"I thought you were an all-time champ," I said. "Not an all-time chump." Then I walked out of the kid's life for good. Or so I thought.

Chapter Seven

The Troubles Begin

I'll tell you, I was pretty down as I made my way to the harbor. I thought the kid and I were close. I thought we had a partnership.

As I went along, I started to get a bad feeling—a really bad feeling. Hades was Trouble with a capital *T*. What was he planning for Herc? Could Herc handle him? Even though Zeus was his old man, Herc was only mortal, after all. Hades was a god. I tried to get them out of my mind. Herc had made his choice. I had done all I could do.

When I got to town, people were running around like crazy, panicking. Chaos everywhere.

"What's up?" I asked a guy.

"Get out of town!" he yelled. "Hades has let all the Titans loose! He's trying to take over Olympus! Kiss your tail good-bye."

"What about Hercules?" I asked. "He can handle it."

"Ha!" said the guy. "Hercules? That wimp. He isn't doing anything at all. Seems like our hero is a zero after all."

Well, I almost had a heart attack. Hercules sitting around while Hades made trouble? That didn't sound like the Herc I knew—unless Meg had something to do with it. I sat down and clutched my head. What a mess. If only Herc had listened to me. . . .

But it wasn't my problem. Not anymore. I stood up and trotted down to the docks. With luck, I could catch a commuter barge back to my island, Idra.

I was just getting my boarding pass when I heard someone yell, "Phil! Wait!"

Would you believe it was Megara? She had some nerve, but she was on Pegasus. Why had he let her ride him?

"Please, Phil," Meg cried. "Hercules needs your help!"

"Why does he need me, when he's got

friends like you?" I said.

"Look, helping Hades was wrong, I admit it," said Meg, jumping off of Pegasus. "I can't explain right now. But quit thinking about me, and think about Herc. He really needs you. You're the only one who can help him. Please!"

I looked at Pegasus, and he nodded.

"Let's go—on or off?" yelled the captain. I waved him to go on without me.

"Okay, what's the deal with Herc?" I asked Meg. Maybe I was a fool, but I still had a soft spot in my heart for the big guy.

"Herc made a deal with Hades," Megara said. "Hades promised him I wouldn't get hurt if Herc gave up his powers."

"He *what*?" I exploded. I couldn't believe my ears. But Megara interrupted me.

"Look, Hercules gave us *both* something we needed," Meg said softly. "Hope. He showed you that you could train a real winner.

"And Herc showed me that he believed in me. Now he has no hope himself. You're the only one who can give it back to him. Phil, if you don't help him, he'll die." Her big blue eyes filled with tears. Heck, I could almost see what the kid saw in her.

"Where is he?" I said.

Pegasus snorted happily. Meg and I climbed on his back and we took off to save the kid.

Chapter Eight

The Battle

We found Herc outside the city. A cyclops was toying with him like a cat with a mouse. The kid was bruised and battered, all the fight knocked out of him.

"Hercules!" I said.

He blinked at me groggily. "Phil."

"C'mon, kid! Fight back!" I said. "You can take this bum. He's a pushover! Look at him, the big one-eyed dope!"

"You were right, Phil," Herc mumbled.

45

"Dreams are for rookies."

"No, no, I was wrong, kid," I said quickly. The goofy ape was closing on us. "You're the one who was right. You said you could go the distance. You *can*. You just have to believe in yourself. *I* believe in you."

Hercules blinked again. At that moment the huge cyclops grabbed Herc and held him in his fist.

"Listen, Herc," I yelled up at him. "You said you weren't like Achilles or Jason or Odysseus, remember? You said you were different. C'mon, kid. Prove it to me. You can do it."

Herc's eyes opened. I caught a glimpse of his old fire.

"Me bite off head!" said the cyclops, lifting Herc.

But Herc grabbed a burning tree trunk and jabbed it in the cyclops's eye!

"Way to go, Herc!" I shouted.

The cyclops screamed and dropped the kid.

46

"Me kill you!" the cyclops shouted. But
he couldn't see, and as we watched, he stag-
gered over the edge of a cliff and fell to his
doom. We all cheered.

47

"Hercules! Watch out!" Meg cried suddenly. An old stone column was about to fall on him! Meg rushed in and pushed him out of the way. The column fell right on top of her instead!

"Meg, no!" Herc yelled, running over to her. Pinned under the column, Meg moaned pitifully. Hercules had given up his strength, but he tried to move the column anyway. Slowly, as Pegasus and I watched in amaze-

ment, Herc managed to move the column. His strength had returned!

I rushed over and pulled Meg free. She had saved Herc's life. That made her all right in *my* book.

"Hades controlled me," Meg told Herc softly. "But he doesn't anymore. He promised you that I wouldn't get hurt. But I did get hurt, so you have your strength back."

"Why did you do this? You didn't have to," Herc said.

"I guess people do crazy things when they're in love," Meg said.

"Oh, Meg, I . . . I," Herc stammered.

"You haven't got much time," Meg said weakly. "You must stop Hades, before it's too late."

"I'll watch over Meg, kid," I said. "Go on. Save the world, like I taught you."

Herc gently laid Meg in my arms. "You're going to be all right," he promised her. "I'll be back soon."

Hercules jumped onto Pegasus's back, and with a flurry of white wings, they were gone.

Chapter Nine

The Battle Is Won

I'm a satyr, not a doctor. But I did what I could to make Meg comfortable. When things quieted down—*if* things quieted down—well, until then, we just had to wait.

Above us the sky was full of black, angry clouds. Huge rolls of thunder and jagged bolts of lightning rained down on us. We could hear volcanos erupting and seas raging and mountains quaking where they stood.

51

But we couldn't tell what was happening on Mount Olympus. We couldn't tell what was happening with the kid.

Meg tried to be brave. The girl had a lot of spunk, I'll give her that. But she was getting weaker and weaker. I wished Herc would wrap things up fast. I told her to hang on, to be brave. But slowly her eyes closed and she went limp. I groaned. What was I going to tell Herc?

Minutes later Pegasus swooped down from the sky. Herc leaped off and ran over to Meg.

"I'm sorry, kid," I told him.

"Meg! No!" Herc shouted. He picked Meg up and kissed her cheek.

"This wasn't supposed to happen," he said.

I felt awful. Pegasus whinnied sadly.

"I'm sorry," I said again. "But some things you just can't change."

Herc looked up. "Yes, I can," he said. Then he hopped back on Pegasus and took off again.

To tell you the truth, I still don't know exactly what Herc did to Hades down in the underworld. It wasn't pretty, I can guess that much. All I know is that after a while Herc came back. He was different. He had a godlike glow.

When Herc kissed Meg, she took a breath and opened her eyes.

It was a miracle! Pegasus and I hugged, then we hugged Herc and Meg, then *they* hugged, and so on. It was a regular hugfest.

"So what happened, kid?" I asked.

Suddenly a lightning bolt blasted out of

nowhere, and a big, billowy cloud formed. Herc held on to Meg tightly as the cloud began to raise them into the sky.

"Hey," I yelled. "You're going nowhere without me." I jumped on Pegasus's back, and together we took off after them.

We got to the great hall at Mount Olympus just in time to see all the gods give Herc a standing ovation. My boy had done me proud!

"Fine work," Zeus said. "You're a true hero! Now, at last, my son, you can come home and take your rightful place on Mount Olympus."

"Father," said Hercules, "this is the moment I've been working so hard for. But . . . a life without Meg—even an immortal life— would be so empty."

The kid took Meg's hand, and she smiled at him.

"I wish to stay on earth with her, Father," said Hercules. "I finally know where I belong."

Zeus looked a little disappointed, if you want to know the truth. But he and Hera seemed to understand. Then everyone kissed good-bye and the cloud that had brought Meg and Herc to Olympus brought them down to earth again.

I don't mind telling you I had tears in my eyes. But the best part of all? My dream came true, too. Zeus put a new cluster of stars in the sky—a portrait of Herc. And nowadays, when people see it, they say, "Hey, that's Phil's boy."

I just love it when they do that!

My Doodle Page: